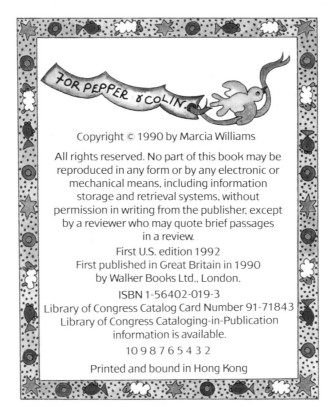

JOSEPH
and his
MAGNIFICENT COAT
OF MANY COLORS

by
Marcia Williams

CANDLEWICK PRESS
CAMBRIDGE, MASSACHUSETTS

There once lived, in the land of Canaan,

a farmer called Jacob.

Jacob had twelve fine sons,

but the one he loved best was Joseph.

HAPPY 17th BIRTHDAY

Jacob gave Joseph a magnificent coat of many colors,

In Joseph's first dream,

he and his brothers were binding corn.

In this dream, Joseph's sheaf rose and stood upright,

and his brothers' sheaves bowed down before it.

In Joseph's second dream,

the sun, the moon, and eleven stars

bowed down before him as though he were king.

Joseph's father believed the dreams meant

We must not forget these dreams.

that Joseph would become a great ruler.

Then, at midday, as the brothers sat down to eat,

they saw a company of Ishmaelites ride over the hill,

their camels loaded with spices to sell in Egypt.

The brothers decided to sell Joseph to the travelers

in exchange for a bag of silver.

Then they dipped Joseph's beautiful coat in blood

and returned home to their father.

Jacob was heartbroken when he saw the coat.

Believing that Joseph had been killed by wild beasts,

he put on sackcloth and mourned his favorite son.

For two years Joseph languished in prison.

The other prisoners liked and respected him,

for he was a wise interpreter of their dreams.

But for Joseph it was a sad and lonely time.

sat puzzling over two strange dreams.

His wise man could not fathom their meaning,

so Joseph was brought out of prison

and asked to interpret them.

"In my first dream," Pharaoh told Joseph,

"I was standing by the River Nile.

when out of the river came seven fat cows.

Then came seven ugly, gaunt cows,

who ate the fat cows but remained thin."

The brothers pleaded with Joseph to enslave

them instead, and set Benjamin free.

Joseph saw then that his brothers had changed.

He knew that they loved Benjamin and their father

and would give their lives for them.

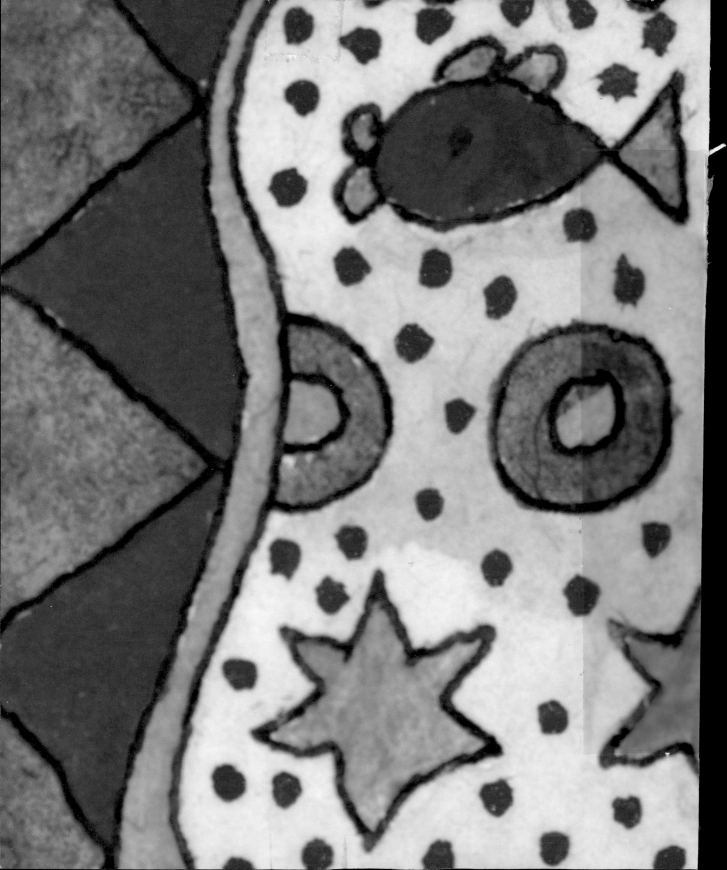